MAGIC CASTLE READERS®

What Do You Do
With a Grumpy Kangaroo?

A book about feelings

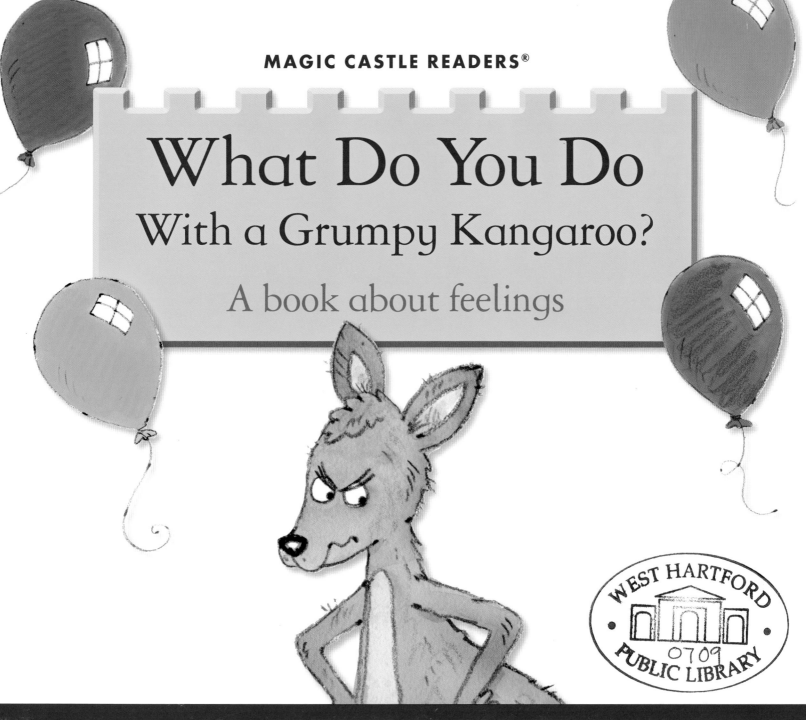

BY JANE BELK MONCURE • ILLUSTRATED BY MERNIE GALLAGHER-COLE

The Child's World

Published by The Child's World®
1980 Lookout Drive • Mankato, MN 56003-1705
800-599-READ • www.childsworld.com

Acknowledgments
The Child's World®: Mary Berendes, Publishing Director
The Design Lab: Design
Jody Jensen Shaffer: Editing

ISBN 9781623235895
LCCN 2013931421

Printed in the United States of America
Mankato, MN
July 2013
PA02177

Did you know...

A library is a magic castle with many Word Windows in it?

What is a Word Window?

If you said, "A book," you're right!

A book is a Word Window because the words and pictures let you look and see many things. Books are your windows to the wide, wide world around you.

The Library
Is a Magic Castle

Come to the Magic Castle
When you are growing tall.
Rows and rows of Word Windows
Line every single wall.
They reach up high,
As high as the sky,
And you'll want to open them all.
For every time you open one,
A new adventure has begun.

Dan opens a Word Window.
Guess what Dan sees.

A grumpy kangaroo. What can Dan do?

"I will try to help Grumpy Kangaroo.
I will be her friend," says Dan.

Dan takes Grumpy Kangaroo to the circus.
He buys her a balloon.

They watch the elephants do tricks.
They watch the ballerinas dance.
They watch the ponies prance.

They see the tumblers tumble.
They see the clowns make funny faces.

Grumpy Kangaroo begins to giggle.

She makes funny faces, too.
She is a happy kangaroo.

Then her balloon pops. She begins to cry.
Now she is a sad kangaroo.
What can Dan do?

Dan buys Sad Kangaroo a new balloon.
Now Kangaroo is a glad kangaroo!

But she drops the string.
The balloon floats away.
Now Kangaroo is a mad kangaroo.

Dan takes Mad Kangaroo to the park.
What does Mad Kangaroo do?

She bumps Dan on the see-saw.
Bump! Bump!

"Bad Kangaroo," says Dan.
Kangaroo says, "I am sorry. I won't bump
you anymore."

"Good Kangaroo," says Dan.
"Let's go down the slide."

Kangaroo gets to the top. It is very high.
She is afraid to go down.

Kangaroo is a scared kangaroo.

Then Dan goes down first.

Now Kangaroo is a brave kangaroo.
Down she goes. Zoom!

Brave Kangaroo says, "Let's ride bikes."
Down the hill they go. Zip!

But Kangaroo goes too fast. She tumbles off her bike. Now Kangaroo is a hurt kangaroo.

What can Dan do? He puts a bandage on
Kangaroo's knee.

Now Kangaroo is sleepy.
She is a sleepy, fussy kangaroo.

Dan puts Kangaroo in bed for a nap.

When Kangaroo wakes up,
she is a joyful, jumpy kangaroo!

"Let's jump rope," says Joyful, Jumpy Kangaroo.
And they do.

Kangaroo keeps on jumping.
She jumps all the way home to the zoo.

Dan closes the Word Window.

Questions and Activities

(Write your answers on a sheet of paper.)

1. In one sentence, tell what this book is about.
   What details does the author use to tell the story?

2. Describe two characters in the story.
   Write two things about each one.

3. Did this story have any words you don't know?
   How can you find out what they mean?

4. Why did the kangaroo not want to go down the slide?
   What made the kangaroo decide to go?

5. Name two things you learned about feelings.
   What else would you like to know?